A Note from Michelle about
THE PENGUIN SKATES

Hi! I'm Michelle Tanner, and I'm nine years old. This year I've got a great New Year's resolution. I'm doing nice things for others. There's just one problem—and it's a big one! Every time I try to do something nice it turns into a disaster. I was supposed to be making people happy. But instead, they're really, really mad!

My family can't even help me with this one. I wish they could because I have a very big family!

There's my dad and my two older sisters, D.J. and Stephanie. But that's not all.

My mom died when I was little. So my uncle Jesse moved in to help Dad take care of us. So did Joey Gladstone. He's my dad's friend from college. It's almost like having three dads. But that's still not all!

First Uncle Jesse got married to Becky Donaldson. Then they had twin boys, Nicky and Alex. The twins are four years old now. And they're so cute.

That's nine people. Our dog, Comet, makes ten. Sure, it gets kind of crazy sometimes. But I wouldn't change it for anything. It's so much fun living in a full house!

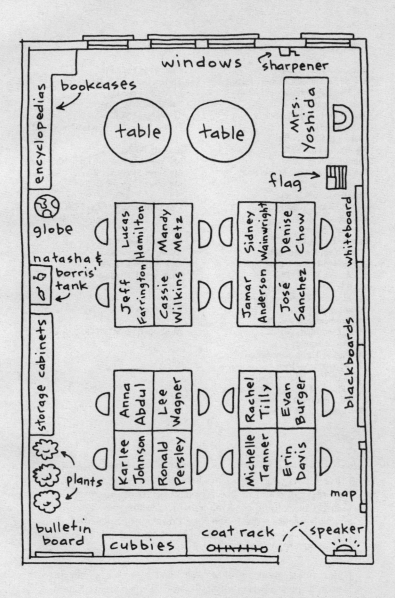

windows   sharpener

bookcases

encyclopedias

table   table

Mrs. Yoshida

flag

globe

natasha & borris' tank

storage cabinets

whiteboard

blackboards

map

| Lucas Farrington Hamilton | Mandy Metz | | Sidney Wainwright | Denise Chow |
| Jeff Farrington | Cassie Wilkins | | Jamar Anderson | José Sanchez |

| Anna Abdul Johnson | Lee Wagner | | Rachel Tilly | Evan Burger |
| Karlee Johnson | Ronald Persley | | Michelle Tanner | Erin Davis |

plants

bulletin board   cubbies   coat rack   speaker

FULL HOUSE™ MICHELLE novels

The Great Pet Project
The Super-Duper Sleepover Party
My Two Best Friends
Lucky, Lucky Day
The Ghost in My Closet
Ballet Surprise
Major League Trouble
My Fourth-Grade Mess
Bunk 3, Teddy and Me
My Best Friend Is a Movie Star!
　(Super Special)
The Big Turkey Escape
The Substitute Teacher
Calling All Planets
I've Got a Secret
How to Be Cool
The Not-So-Great Outdoors
My Ho-Ho-Horrible Christmas
My Almost Perfect Plan
April Fools!
My Life Is a Three-Ring Circus
Welcome to My Zoo
The Problem with Pen Pals
Merry Christmas, World!
Tap Dance Trouble
The Fastest Turtle in the West
The Baby-sitting Boss
The Wish I Wish I Never Wished
Pigs, Pies, and Plenty of Problems
If I Were President
How to Meet a Superstar

Unlucky in Lunch
There's Gold in My Backyard!
Field Day Foul-Up
Smile and Say "Woof!"
The Penguin Skates
For the Birds (Coming in March 2001)

Activity Books
My Awesome Holiday Friendship Book
My Super Sleepover Book
My Year of Fun Book

FULL HOUSE™ SISTERS

Two on the Town
One Boss Too Many
And the Winner Is . . .
How to Hide a Horse
Problems in Paradise
Will You Be My Valentine?
Let's Put On a Show!
Baby-sitters & Company

Available from MINSTREL Books

FULL HOUSE™

Michelle
and Friends

THE PENGUIN SKATES

Judy Katschke

A Parachute Press Book

Published by POCKET BOOKS
New York   London   Toronto   Sydney   Singapore

A MINSTREL PAPERBACK *Original*

A Minstrel Book published by
POCKET BOOKS, a division of Simon & Schuster, Inc.
1230 Avenue of the Americas, New York, NY 10020

A PARACHUTE PRESS BOOK

Copyright © and ™ 2001 by Warner Bros.

FULL HOUSE, characters, names and all related indicia are trademarks of Warner Bros. © 2001.

ISBN: 0-671-04201-7

First Minstrel Books printing January 2001

10 9 8 7 6 5 4 3 2 1

A MINSTREL BOOK and colophon are registered trademarks of Simon & Schuster, Inc.

Printed in the U.S.A.

Chapter 1

♥ "Happy New Year, everybody!" nine-year-old Michelle Tanner cried. It was Monday—the first day back from winter break. All the children in Mrs. Yoshida's fourth-grade class were hanging up their coats.

"What's so happy about going back to school?" Jeff Farrington asked. "It was more fun watching cartoons for a whole week."

"You watch cartoons every day, anyway!" José Sanchez joked.

Jamar Anderson slipped his ski jacket onto a top hook. "I stayed up until midnight on

New Year's Eve. My dad bought us all goofy hats and noisemakers."

"We had noisemakers, too," Denise Chow groaned. "My baby cousins."

It's going to be a great year! Michelle thought as she hung up her jacket. She had gotten a new pair of ice skates for Christmas. And she had made a brand-new New Year's resolution.

But her best friend, Mandy Metz, didn't seem so happy.

"Oh, no," Mandy groaned. Her long red coat was draped over her arm. "No top hooks left. Now my new coat will drag on the floor."

"What are you going to do?" Michelle's other best friend, Cassie Wilkins, asked.

Michelle grabbed her own jacket off a top hook. "Take my hook, Mandy," she said. "Please!"

Mandy and Cassie looked at each other and giggled.

2

"What?" Michelle asked.

"You've been doing nice things all morning," Mandy replied.

"First you gave me the window seat on the bus," Cassie said. "And then, when Sidney Wainwright sneezed, you walked all the way up the aisle to give her your last tissue. What's up, Michelle?"

"It's my New Year's resolution," Michelle replied. "From now on I'm going to do nice things for people."

"But you're always nice," Cassie said. "That time I forgot my lunch, you gave me half of your tuna sandwich. And that was *last* year."

True. Michelle always liked doing nice things for other people. But this year she wanted her good deeds to be special. Extra special!

"My resolution has got to be more than just window seats and tuna fish," Michelle tapped her chin as she thought. "But what?"

"Don't worry, Michelle," Cassie said. "You'll think of something."

Mandy cleared her throat. "Michelle isn't the only one with a resolution," she said. "I made one, too."

"You did?" Michelle asked excitedly. "What is it?"

"To clean my room every day," Mandy announced. "My mom is right—it's a total mess."

"Clean your room?" Cassie repeated. "That was your resolution last year."

"It was?" Mandy gave a little shrug. "I guess I forgot."

Michelle giggled. She was about to stick her gloves into her coat pocket when someone brushed against her. She turned to see Rachel Tilly holding a black jacket with fake fur trim. It looked brand new.

"Hello, *Michelle*," Rachel said.

Rachel was not Michelle's favorite classmate. Michelle smiled at her anyway. "Hi, Rachel. How was your winter break?"

"Awesome!" Rachel declared. She reached out and hung her jacket right on top of Michelle's. "First we went skiing in Colorado. Every night we drank hot cocoa and went on a sleigh ride—with bells on the horses. And we stayed in a log cabin that had a huge fireplace."

Michelle wasn't surprised. Rachel's father was a famous baker who owned a chain of bakeries all over the country. They always took great vacations.

"Am I lucky or what?" Rachel asked.

"You sure are," Mandy said. "But we *all* had fun over winter break."

"Yeah," Cassie said. "I went to the circus—"

"And for Christmas," Rachel interrupted, "I got video games and a big TV for my room. What did you get?"

Cassie and Mandy didn't answer. But

Michelle wanted to tell Rachel about her favorite Christmas present. "My dad gave me a pair of cool ice skates," Michelle said excitedly.

Rachel flipped her super-long hair over her shoulder. "Big deal," she said. "I get new skates every year—for my *private* lessons."

The words hit Michelle like a ton of snowballs. Michelle was proud of her skates. How could Rachel be so mean?

"Forget about it, Michelle," Cassie said as Rachel walked off toward her desk. "What do you expect from her?"

Mandy began to giggle. "Hey, Michelle," she said. "I just thought of an extra-hard New Year's resolution for you!"

Michelle turned to Mandy. "What?"

"Make friends with Rachel Tilly!" Mandy laughed.

"That's not just hard," Cassie said. "That's *impossible!*"

Mandy and Cassie gave each other high-fives. But Michelle wasn't laughing. Maybe her best friends had a point. . . .

Ever since we both ran for class president, Rachel and I have been competing with each other, Michelle thought. Maybe it's finally time to be friends.

"Cassie? Mandy?" Michelle said. "Is it okay to have two resolutions?"

Mandy whistled. "I can't even keep one!"

"Michelle?" Cassie asked slowly. "You're not really thinking of making friends with Rachel, are you?"

"I know it's a challenge," Michelle admitted. "But anything is possible in a new year, right?"

"Well, good luck, Michelle," Cassie said.

Michelle smiled. "Thanks. With two resolutions, I'm going to need it!"

Chapter 2

♥ "Class, let's get started," Mrs. Yoshida called from her desk. "Everyone in their seats."

Michelle carried her backpack to her desk. Something felt nice and warm inside it. Michelle knew it was a thermos filled with her dad's homemade creamy portobello mushroom soup.

"By the way, boys and girls," Mrs. Yoshida said. "I got a note from the principal's office. Lucas won't be in school today. He got sick over winter break."

Michelle glanced at Lucas's empty desk. Poor Lucas, she thought. I wish there was something I could do for him.

Then Michelle remembered the hot soup in her backpack. I know, I can bring Lucas a bowl of soup after school. Soup is great when you're sick. And Lucas lives only three blocks from me.

Michelle turned to face her friends. "Cassie, Mandy, I just thought of my first really good deed," she whispered. She gave them a thumbs-up sign. "All systems go!"

"What's wrong with Lucas, Michelle?" Michelle's dad, Danny, asked in the kitchen that afternoon. Michelle had raced straight home from school. Danny poured a ladle of steaming hot mushroom soup into a bowl.

"No clue, Dad," Michelle said. "But whatever it is, he'll feel a lot better after he eats your soup."

Danny popped a plastic lid on top of the bowl. "Tell Lucas there's more where this came from. I got carried away and made three big pots."

"Three?" Michelle's eyes lit up. "Did you say *three?*"

Danny nodded. "Yeah, why?"

"Dad, I just got *another* idea," Michelle said. "We can start a soup kitchen right here in our house—for hungry people!"

"Whoa, Michelle." Danny shook his head and laughed. "One good deed at a time, okay?"

"Okay, Dad," Michelle sighed. She slipped a soup spoon into her pocket. Then Danny held the door as she carefully carried the bowl outside.

Michelle walked the three blocks to the Hamiltons' house. The smell of the hot soup drifted straight up to her nose. She shut her eyes and took a big, long whiff. "Mmmm!"

"Beep, beep!" a voice shouted.

Michelle's eyes popped open. She saw Rachel and Sidney Rollerblading down the block at full speed.

"Out of our way!" Rachel demanded.

Michelle was about to jump to the side when she remembered her second resolution. If she was going to become friends with Rachel, she had to *talk* to Rachel.

Rachel and Sidney slowed down. They stopped in front of Michelle.

"Hi," Michelle said with a bright smile.

"Why didn't you move?" Rachel asked. "We were just on a roll!"

"On a roll!" Sidney giggled. "That's funny, Rachel. Especially since we were Roller—"

"It wasn't a joke," Rachel said, interrupting her best friend.

Michelle took a deep breath. If that was how Rachel treated people she liked, making friends with her wasn't going to be easy. But she had made her resolution, and she was going to stick to it.

I know, Michelle thought. I'll compliment Rachel. Everybody likes compliments.

Michelle noticed the red velvet scrunchy around Rachel's ponytail. "That's a nice scrunchy you're wearing, Rachel," she said brightly. "Did you get it for Christmas?"

Rachel stared at Michelle. "What do you want?" she demanded.

"Huh?" Michelle asked.

"You never say nice things about my clothes." Rachel narrowed her eyes. "I bet you want to get a velvet scrunchy just like mine. So you can *copy* me!"

"No." Michelle shook her head. "I was just being nice. It's part of my New Year's resolution."

"New Year's resolution?" Rachel repeated.

"Yes, see?" Michelle held up the bowl. "I'm bringing Lucas hot soup so he'll feel better. I'm doing nice things for people."

Rachel stared at Michelle as if she didn't believe her. Sidney was staring at Michelle, too. But in a nice way.

"Those are pretty earrings, Michelle," Sidney said.

"Thanks," Michelle answered. She was wearing her swingy silver earrings with the turquoise beads.

"Let's go, Sidney," Rachel said. She tugged at her friend's elbow. "We're supposed to skate all the way to the park, remember?"

Michelle moved to the side as Rachel and Sidney skated by. She watched Rachel's long ponytail bounce behind her. That didn't go very well, Michelle thought. But I'm not giving up on Rachel. Not yet.

Michelle walked the rest of the way to Lucas's house. She stepped up to the door and rang the bell. Mrs. Hamilton opened the door and smiled.

"Hello," Michelle said. "My name is Michelle. I'm in Lucas's class at school."

"Oh, I know you," Mrs. Hamilton said. "You're the fourth-grade class president. I saw your picture in the school paper."

Michelle lifted the bowl. "Mrs. Yoshida told us that Lucas is sick," she said. "So I brought over some of my dad's homemade soup."

"Well, isn't that sweet," Mrs. Hamilton said. "Lucas loves soup. Especially the kind with the little stars and letters floating around in it."

Michelle followed Mrs. Hamilton into the house. After finding a tray in the kitchen, Mrs. Hamilton led Michelle up the stairs.

"Lucas, honey," Mrs. Hamilton said as they walked into Lucas's bedroom. "You have a visitor. And she brought you something."

Lucas groaned. He was lying in bed with the covers up to his chin. "Is it homework?"

Lucas sank under the covers. "I don't feel like doing homework today."

"It's not homework, Lucas," Michelle said. "It's soup!"

"Soup?" Lucas began to sit up. "The kind with the little letters floating around in it?"

"Better," Michelle declared. "It's home-made. I liked it so much that I wanted to share it with you. It's part of my New Year's resolution to do nice things for people."

"Oh, Lucas has a New Year's resolution, too," Mrs. Hamilton said. "Not to pick at his scabs."

"Maaaaa!" Lucas blushed.

Mrs. Hamilton placed the tray in front of Lucas. Then Michelle took the lid off the bowl and gave Lucas the spoon.

"Smells good." Lucas shrugged. He lifted a spoonful of steaming hot soup into his mouth. His eyes widened as he quickly swallowed it.

"Well?" Michelle asked. "What do you think?"

"Bleccch!" Lucas dropped the spoon onto the tray. He clapped a hand over his mouth and began to gag!

"Lucas?" Mrs. Hamilton said. "Is something wrong?"

"What kind of soup is this?" Lucas gasped.

"Mushroom soup," Michelle answered. "With extra mushrooms."

"Extra m-m-mushrooms?" Lucas jumped out of bed. "I don't ever want to see another mushroom as long as I live!"

Michelle watched in horror as Lucas ran from the room.

"I—I was only trying to be nice, Mrs. Hamilton!" she cried. "What did I do wrong?"

Chapter 3

♥ "Did he really turn green?" Cassie asked Michelle the next morning before class. They were standing by their desks, waiting for Mrs. Yoshida.

"Practically," Michelle sighed. "Mrs. Hamilton told me Lucas got sick eating too many slices of mushroom pizza. Now if he even looks at a mushroom, it makes him sick."

"Bummer," Mandy said.

Michelle shook her head. "That mushroom soup was a bad idea."

"It was not," Cassie insisted. "It's the

thought that counts. Like when your grandmother gives you an itchy sweater for your birthday!"

"Besides," Mandy said. She pointed to the big calendar on the classroom wall. "You have another three hundred and fifty-nine days to do something nice for someone. So relax!"

"I can't!" Michelle declared. "I have to do something really nice for someone. Right now!"

Michelle sat down at her desk. She tried to think of another good deed. Maybe I can walk Mrs. Yoshida's dog, she thought. But then she remembered that her teacher only had a bird.

Michelle slumped down in her seat. Erin Davis and Anna Abdul were standing in the aisle, talking loudly.

"I can't believe it, Erin!" Anna said. "I checked out the class job list, and I have to clean out Boris and Natasha's cage every day for the next week. And it's during recess!"

Michelle shuddered. She loved the class's pet mice. But like everyone else, she hated cleaning out their cage.

"Hey, it's a gross job," Erin said with a shrug. "But somebody's got to do it."

"But Denise brought in her electronic yo-yo today," Anna complained. "She said she'd let everyone play with it during recess. Now I can't!"

Michelle felt a little sorry for Anna. She knew Anna really wanted to play with that yo-yo.

Maybe there's something I can do for Anna, she thought. Something nice . . . something really, *really* nice! Michelle's eyes lit up.

"Anna!" Michelle called. "Why don't you let me clean out the cage for you today?"

Anna's head snapped around. She left Erin and walked over to Michelle's desk. "What did you just say?"

"I said, 'Why don't you let me clean out Boris and Natasha's cage today?'" Michelle replied.

"That's what I thought you said." Anna tilted her head. "Are you feeling okay, Michelle?"

"I feel great," Michelle said. "I just want to do nice things for people. Besides, I got to try out the yo-yo at the mall last week."

The door opened, and Mrs. Yoshida walked into the classroom.

"Should we tell Mrs. Yoshida?" Anna asked.

Michelle gave it some thought. Mrs. Yoshida always spent recess in the teachers' lounge while the recess monitors watched all the classes. She would never know if Michelle took Anna's job. Then Anna could get all the credit, and Michelle would be doing something extra-nice!

"No," Michelle said, shaking her head. "As

long as the cage gets cleaned, Mrs. Yoshida won't mind."

"Thanks, Michelle," Anna said with a little jump. "You're the best!"

Michelle leaned back and smiled. The mushroom soup disaster was history. Now all it took to be nice . . . were two little white mice!

For the first time ever, Michelle couldn't wait to clean the mouse cage. She waited patiently through social studies, English, and lunch. When it was time for recess, Anna followed the others out to the school yard. Michelle stayed behind in the classroom with Cassie and Mandy.

"Thanks for helping me, you guys," Michelle told her friends.

"No problem," Cassie said. "The boys will probably hog the yo-yo, anyway."

Mandy pulled a candy bar from her jeans

pocket. "Here's something the boys won't get their hands on," she said. "An extra-chewy, super-gooey Nutty Buddy bar. Anyone want a piece?"

"No way, Mandy." Michelle rolled up her sleeves. "We've got work to do."

The girls marched to the back of the classroom where the mouse cage stood. Boris and Natasha were lazily lying beside a pile of half-eaten cabbage.

"They look bored," Cassie said.

"You would be, too, if you ate nothing but vegetables," Mandy said. She turned to Michelle. "I haven't had my turn cleaning the cage yet. Where do we start?"

Michelle had cleaned out the cage before, so she knew what to do. She pulled on a pair of rubber gloves. Then she found a smaller empty cage under the table.

"First we put Boris and Natasha in the small cage," Michelle explained. She pointed to a bottle of Squirt n' Scrub and a roll of paper towels. "Then we scrub out the big cage with that stuff."

"This is worse than cleaning my room," Mandy complained. She turned to leave. "Maybe I will play with that yo-yo—"

"No, wait!" Michelle interrupted. "You can hold the small cage while Cassie and I clean out the big cage."

"It's a deal," Mandy said.

Michelle carefully opened the cage door and reached in. She gently grabbed Boris and placed him inside the smaller cage. Then she did the same with Natasha. Michelle fastened the lock on the door and handed the cage to Mandy.

"So far, so good," Mandy said. She held the cage in one hand and the candy bar in the other.

Michelle sprayed the big cage with some Squirt n' Scrub.

"Eeek!" Mandy screamed.

Michelle whirled around. Boris and Natasha were nibbling on Mandy's fingers through the cage!

"Michelle! Cassie!" Mandy whined. "They're licking the chocolate off my fingers. Gross!"

Michelle ran over to Mandy. "Don't move," she said, reaching out for the cage. "Whatever you do, don't—"

CRASH!

Michelle screamed as the cage fell to the floor. The little door snapped open, and the two mice scurried out.

"Oh, no!" Michelle cried. "Boris and Natasha are getting away!"

Chapter
4

♥ "Get them!" Michelle cried.

Michelle, Cassie, and Mandy chased the little mice all around the classroom.

"They're heading for the door!" Cassie shouted.

Boris and Natasha scampered out of the classroom and into the hallway. They dashed past the trophy case, the nutrition mural, and finally the water fountain, where a girl was taking a drink.

Michelle gasped. The girl was Anna Abdul!

Anna screamed when Boris and Natasha ran

through her legs. She turned to Michelle. "What did you do, Michelle?" she demanded. "Why are Boris and Natasha out of their cage?"

"I can't explain now, Anna," Michelle said. "Just help us catch them, please!"

The four girls went faster as they chased Boris and Natasha down the hall and around a corner.

"They can't get too far!" Mandy said.

"Why not?" Anna asked.

"They don't have hall passes," Mandy joked.

Michelle rolled her eyes as they skidded around a corner. "This is not the time for jokes, Mandy. This is—"

Michelle never finished her sentence. She screeched to a stop. Boris and Natasha were squeezing under a door marked TEACHERS' LOUNGE.

"Why?" Michelle cried as she stared at the door. "Of all the doors in this school why did they have to pick the teachers' lounge? Why? Why? *Why?*"

"Maybe the teachers won't notice Boris and Natasha," Cassie said. "Maybe—"

"It's a mouse!" a voice behind the door shrieked.

"Two of them!" another voice cried.

"Eeeeeek!"

"I think . . . they saw them," Anna said slowly.

The screaming stopped, and the door flew open. Mrs. Yoshida stood in front of the girls, holding Boris by his tail in one hand and Natasha in the other hand.

Michelle glanced past Mrs. Yoshida into the lounge. Tables and plates of food were over-turned. Mrs. Barnett, another fourth-grade teacher, was standing on a chair.

Michelle's mouth felt dry. She thought Mrs. Yoshida would scold her. But instead the teacher looked straight at Anna.

"Anna?" Mrs. Yoshida said. "You were cleaning out the cage. Can you explain this?"

Anna opened her mouth to speak, but Michelle jumped in front of her.

"I cleaned out the cage today, Mrs. Yoshida," Michelle admitted. "I offered to do Anna's job for her."

"And I dropped the cage, Mrs. Yoshida," Mandy said. "It was my fault."

Boris and Natasha squeaked and swung back and forth. Mrs. Yoshida stepped out of the teachers' lounge. She did not look pleased.

"It was your responsibility, Anna," Mrs. Yoshida said quietly. "If you wanted to give your job to Michelle, you both should have spoken to me."

Michelle heaved a big sigh. "I'm sorry, Mrs. Yoshida," she said.

"So am I," Anna said.

"I know you are," Mrs. Yoshida said. "But I want you both to clean out the mouse cage today."

"But Mrs. Yoshida," Michelle said. "Recess is almost over."

"After school," Mrs. Yoshida added. "Now go join the others in the school yard."

"Thanks a lot, Michelle," Anna whispered.

Michelle gulped. "I—I was only trying to be nice," she whispered back.

Outside in the school yard Anna told Erin about the mice. And Erin told Denise. And Denise told José. And José told Jamar—until everyone in Mrs. Yoshida's class was whispering about it.

Michelle wanted to disappear!

"Don't worry, Michelle," Cassie said. "It wasn't your fault."

"Yeah, Michelle," Mandy said. "Blame it on the extra-chewy, super-gooey Nutty Buddy!"

"Meet you at the swings," Cassie told Michelle.

Michelle watched her two best friends walk away. Why couldn't she do something nice for someone—just once—without it going horribly wrong?

She was about to follow Cassie and Mandy when Sidney came over. "You're wearing my favorite earrings again, Michelle," Sidney said. "I wish I had a pair like them."

"You do?" Michelle asked. Then she had an idea. She began to undo her earrings. "Here, Sidney," she said. "You take them."

"For keeps?" Sidney gasped. "Are you sure?"

Michelle handed the earrings to Sidney. "They're yours."

"Thanks, Michelle!" Sidney cried. "You are so nice!"

Well, at least *somebody* thinks so, Michelle thought as Sidney ran off.

And what could go wrong with a pair of earrings?

"You look exhausted, Michelle," Danny said at dinner that night.

"And you smell like Squirt n' Scrub," Michelle's thirteen-year-old sister, Stephanie, added.

Michelle sat in her usual seat at the big kitchen table. The table was big because there were nine people living in the Tanner house. There were Michelle, Stephanie, and their dad, plus Michelle's eighteen-year-old sister, D.J. Uncle Jesse and Aunt Becky lived on the third floor with their four-year-old twin sons, Nicky and Alex. And last but not least, there was Danny's best friend, Joey Gladstone. He lived in the basement of their very full house.

And Michelle couldn't forget the family's golden retriever, Comet. Or her cute little guinea pig, Sunny.

31

"Are we having mushroom soup *again?*" D.J. asked as she stared at the soup bowls set on the table.

"Aren't those pots empty yet, Danny?" Uncle Jesse joked.

"Oh, come on, you guys," Danny said. "You love my creamy mushroom soup. Besides, that's not the whole meal. I've got a hot tuna casserole in the oven."

"A tuna casserole?" Joey asked, scratching his chin. "Don't you make that recipe with—"

"Mushroom soup." Danny nodded. "Okay, so I went a little over the top."

Aunt Becky turned to Michelle. "Should I pour some soup into your bowl, honey?" she asked.

"No thanks, Aunt Becky," Michelle said. "I'm not very hungry today."

Danny placed a hand on Michelle's forehead. "You're not getting sick, are you?"

"Just sick of my New Year's resolution,"

Michelle admitted. "So far it's a total bust. And it's only the beginning of January!"

"What you need is some cheering up, Michelle," Joey said. "And I have just the answer."

"You do?" Michelle asked.

"My agent called today," Joey said. "He told me that I was chosen to host the Yuks on Ice show at the Diamond Rink this Saturday night."

"What's Yuks on Ice?" Stephanie asked.

"Is it yucky?" Nicky asked.

"No." Joey smiled. "It's an event where comedians like myself get to skate for hundreds of people. It's going to be huge!"

"That's great, Joey," Michelle said. "But what does it have to do with me?"

"I'm glad you asked," Joey said with a wink. "The Yuks need a kid to pick up the flowers and teddy bears that people toss on the ice after each performance. You're a good skater," he added. "What do you say?"

For just a moment Michelle forgot all about her New Year's resolutions. Instead she thought about the brand-new ice skates she got for Christmas.

"Thanks, Joey!" Michelle said with a grin. "I say *yes!*"

Chapter
5

♥ "I can't believe you're going to be in a real ice show, Michelle," Mandy said the next day after school. She and Cassie were at the Diamond Rink to help Michelle practice. They were all wearing sweaters, jeans, scarves, and gloves.

"Oh, I believe it," Cassie said, pulling on her skates. "I once saw Michelle do a figure eight!"

Michelle looked up from tying her skates. "It was more like a figure seven," she said. "But thanks, anyway."

When their skates were tied, the three friends hobbled out of the locker room and toward the huge skating rink.

Michelle loved the Diamond Rink. It had rows of bleachers all around the ice and a high ceiling decorated with colorful banners and flags.

"This place is packed," Mandy said.

Michelle, Mandy, and Cassie stood at the rail and watched the skaters. Kids and adults dressed in colorful sweaters and scarves whizzed by. Some were skating alone, and others were skating hand in hand. A few skaters gripped the rail as they tried to learn.

But there was one skater in the middle of the rink who Michelle recognized at once— Rachel.

"Just our luck," Mandy sighed. She turned away from the rink. "Anybody for hot chocolate?"

"No," Michelle said. "Let's watch her skate."

Michelle rested her elbows on the rail as she watched Rachel glide gracefully across the ice. Her long hair was tied up in a bun and crowned with a green velvet scrunchy. She was wearing a white turtleneck sweater, white tights, and a short green velvet skirt with snowflakes on it. Watching Rachel closely was a woman in a blue sweat suit and black skates.

"That's probably Rachel's teacher," Cassie said. "For her private lessons."

Michelle could see that the lessons had paid off. Rachel was doing all sorts of fancy things on the ice—even skating with one leg raised behind her. At one point Rachel crouched down into a sitting position and began spinning on one skate!

"She's doing a sit-spin!" Cassie cried. "Do you know how hard that is?"

"I hate to admit it," Mandy said, "but Rachel is pretty good."

Michelle shook her head. "She's not just good. She's *awesome!*"

The teacher left Rachel alone to practice.

"Come on," Michelle said. "Let's go over and say hi."

Michelle, Mandy, and Cassie skated over to Rachel.

"Nice skating, Rachel," Michelle said. "You're good enough to be in a show."

"A show? That is my biggest dream!" Rachel clasped her hands. "I want to wear velvet and rhinestones and feathers and skate in the spotlight. People will cheer for me and call my name: Ra-chel! Ra-chel! Ra-chel!" She bowed to an imaginary audience.

Wow, Michelle thought. Rachel really wants to be in a show. Too bad she can't have my job on Saturday night. . . .

Hey, wait a minute! If I give my job to

Rachel, I'll be doing something nice for her. Something really, *really* nice!

"Um, Rachel?" Michelle asked. "My dad's best friend, Joey, is hosting an ice show on Saturday night. And he needs someone to pick up the flowers and the teddy bears."

Michelle could hear Mandy and Cassie gasp.

"And?" Rachel asked.

"And," Michelle went on, "I was supposed to do it. But I think you'd do a better job. Do you want to do it?"

Rachel skated closer to Michelle and looked her straight in the eye. "What's the catch?" she asked.

"What do you mean?" Michelle asked.

"Are you hoping I fall on the ice and make a fool of myself in front of hundreds of people?" Rachel asked. She planted her hands on her hips. "Well, are you?"

Michelle couldn't believe her ears. The last

thing she wanted to be was mean! "No way!" she insisted. "I just want to do something nice. Something really, *really* nice."

Rachel was silent as she stared at Michelle. "Will my name be in the program?" she demanded.

"I'll tell Joey to make sure it is," Michelle promised.

"Will I have my own dressing room?" Rachel asked next.

"I don't know about that," Michelle said. "You might have to share it with some of the skating stars."

"Stars?" Rachel gasped. "You mean like Svetlana the Russian Ice Queen?"

"More like Harvey the Rubber Chicken King," Mandy said.

Cassie gave Mandy a sharp nudge.

"There will be lots of good skaters that night," Michelle said. "So what do you say? Will you do it?"

Rachel tilted her head. Then she smiled. "I'll do it."

"Great!" Michelle called as Rachel skated back over to her instructor.

"What was *that* all about, Michelle?" Mandy asked.

"Yeah," Cassie said. "You're supposed to be the flower and teddy bear girl!"

"I *was* the flower and teddy bear girl," Michelle corrected them. "Mandy, Cassie, don't you see? Now I'll be carrying out both of my resolutions—to do nice things for other people and to make friends with Rachel!"

Michelle couldn't wait to tell her family about her super-good deed. But the first thing she had to do when she got home was feed Comet.

"It's fun doing nice things for people, Comet," Michelle said as she unclasped the heavy bag of dog food.

Comet barked as he wagged his big fluffy tail. He licked his mouth as he stared at the bag of Yappy Yummies.

Michelle was about to tip the bag over Comet's dish when Joey walked into the kitchen.

"Hi, Joey," Michelle said. "Wait until you hear my great news!"

"Hey!" Joey replied. "I have great news for you, too!"

"You first," Michelle said.

"I just came back from a meeting with the Yuks committee," Joey said. "They want you to wear a special costume on Saturday night."

"You mean a velvet costume with rhine-stones and feathers?" Michelle asked. Rachel would love that, she thought.

"Nope," Joey said. He began to giggle. "It's—a penguin suit!"

Penguin? Michelle lost her grip on the bag.

A shower of dog food clattered to the floor. Comet barked excitedly as he began munching on the food.

"Joey!" Michelle cried. "Did you say a *penguin suit?*"

"Yup," Joey said, beaming. "You know. Ice. Penguin. Get it?"

Michelle got it, but she didn't want it. "Joey, I—"

"And that's not all," Joey went on. "At the very end of the show, you get a cream pie in your face courtesy of yours truly!"

"C-c-cream pie?" Michelle stammered.

"Imagine it." Joey squeezed Michelle's shoulders. "You'll be the biggest gag in the whole show!"

"But Joey," Michelle squeaked. "I'm not going to be the flower and teddy bear girl. I gave my job to Rachel Tilly!"

"Really?" Joey asked. "Why?"

"Because she's a great skater, and I wanted

to do something nice for her," Michelle explained. "But—"

"That's really sweet, Michelle," Joey interrupted. "Just make sure you tell her about our new idea," he said. "See you!" Then he left the kitchen.

Michelle fell back against the counter. This was worse than the soup. And much worse than the mice!

"Oh, Comet," Michelle groaned. "Rachel thought I wanted her to make a fool of herself in front of hundreds of people. And now she *will!*"

Chapter
6

♥   "A penguin suit?" Mandy laughed in the school yard the next morning. "Are you serious?"

Michelle nodded sadly. She had just told Mandy and Cassie about Joey's idea.

"I can't get over the cream pie!" Cassie giggled. "Too bad it can't be Mr. Tilly's cream puffs!"

Michelle stared at her friends as they laughed. They just didn't get it. "It's not funny, you guys. Now I have to break the news to Rachel. She's going to think I planned it all along."

"When are you going to talk to her?" Cassie asked.

Michelle saw Rachel sitting on a nearby swing. "I'd better do it right now," she said. "And get it over with."

The three friends walked over to the swings. Michelle opened her mouth to speak, but Rachel beat her to it.

"Hi, Michelle!" Rachel said. "I told my parents about Saturday night, and they are so proud. My father promised to bake me anything I wanted. I asked for a banana cream pie!"

Cream pie?

Michelle gulped as she imagined Rachel with whipped cream dripping down her face.

"Um, Rachel?" Michelle said. "There's something I have to tell you. It's about Saturday night."

Rachel began to swing faster. "I already

know what time the show starts. I saw an ad for it in the newspaper."

Michelle felt like she was going to burst! "It's not about the time, Rachel," she said.

"Then what?" Rachel called down from the swing.

"Joey told me that—"

"Michelle!" a voice called out.

Michelle turned to see Sidney running toward them. Her face was streaked with tears.

"What's the matter, Sidney?" Michelle asked.

Sidney shoved Michelle's earrings into her hands. "Take your stupid earrings back!" she sobbed.

"Stupid?" Michelle cried. "I thought you wanted them."

"I did," Sidney sniffed. She pulled back her hair. "Until they made my earlobes turn green!"

47

Michelle, Mandy, and Cassie leaned over to examine Sidney's ears.

"They're green, all right," Mandy said.

"Oooh!" Sidney cried.

"I don't get it," Michelle said. "I wore the earrings, and it didn't happen to me."

"That's because you're not allergic to them!" Sidney explained. "My mother took me to my allergy doctor last night, and he told me I was."

Michelle knew that Sidney was allergic to practically everything. But she'd had no idea Sidney would be allergic to her earrings!

"They're itching like crazy." Sidney began tugging at her earlobes. "Thanks a lot, Michelle!"

Michelle stared at the earrings in her hand. "I—I was just trying to be nice," she stammered.

Rachel jumped off the swing. "Come on, Sidney," she said. "Let's go to the school nurse. Maybe she can stop the itching."

Michelle watched Rachel and Sidney leave. "Another good deed gone wrong," she muttered, shaking her head. "And I still haven't told Rachel about the penguin suit."

During class, Michelle worried about Rachel and the penguin suit. She barely heard a word Mrs. Yoshida said. If I don't tell Rachel soon, Michelle thought, I'll miss the whole day of school! She decided to write Rachel a note.

While Mrs. Yoshida erased the board for the next lesson, Michelle wrote Rachel's note on a piece of paper:

Rachel,
  Surprise! You're going to wear a penguin suit on Saturday night! Isn't that funny?
                                        Your friend,
                                        Michelle

* * *

Michelle folded the note into a tiny square. She was about to pass it to Rachel, who was sitting right next to her, when Mrs. Yoshida looked in their direction. Michelle stuck the note under her notebook.

"Okay, class," Mrs. Yoshida said. "Today we're going to talk about the Antarctic. Does anyone know what kind of animals we find there?"

"Frozen ones!" Jeff Farrington called out.

Mrs. Yoshida shook her head as the class giggled. She pulled down a map of the Antarctic. On it were pictures of exotic animals, fish, and—

"Penguins!" Michelle gasped under her breath.

Mrs. Yoshida grabbed her pointer and tapped a black and white penguin. "Anybody know what this guy is called?" she asked.

Most of the kids called out, "Penguin!"

"They are soooo cute," Denise said.

"They look like they're wearing tuxedos!" Jamar added.

Rachel's hand flew up in the air. "Ewww, penguins are not cute!" she exclaimed. "I saw one in the zoo once, and boy, did he smell."

"I'll bet they don't *all* smell," Denise argued.

"Yes, they *do!*" Rachel snapped.

Michelle crumpled the note and sank into her seat. There was no way she could tell Rachel about the penguin suit now. This was getting worse and worse! She had only wanted to be nice to Rachel so they could be friends. But Rachel hated penguins.

And if Michelle didn't do something quick, Rachel would hate her, too!

Chapter
7

♥ "Joey?" Michelle called. She plopped her backpack on the living room couch. "Are you home?"

"In the kitchen, Michelle," Joey called back.

Michelle had made a decision in school that day. She couldn't bring herself to tell Rachel about the penguin suit. The only way to solve her problem was to change Joey's mind about making Rachel wear it.

Michelle walked through the living room and into the kitchen. There she found Joey, blowing up a pile of whoopee cushions.

"I'm going to put these on the seats at the Yuks meeting tonight as a joke," Joey said. "Good thing I saved them from last Thanksgiving."

"Um, Joey—" Michelle started to say.

Joey pressed on a cushion, and it made a loud sound. "Did you tell Rachel about her costume?" he asked.

"Not yet," Michelle said. She smiled widely. "But that's because I had the most fantastic idea. Why don't you have Rachel skate as another bird?"

"Another bird?" Joey asked.

"Yes—like a beautiful swan," Michelle flapped her arms gracefully in the air. "Or a magnificent peacock!"

"No way," Joey said, shaking his head.

Michelle's shoulders dropped. "Why not?"

"Because peacocks and swans are not funny," Joey said. "Penguins are."

Michelle opened her mouth to speak, but nothing came out.

"It's all set, Michelle," Joey said. "The penguin skates."

It was more than Michelle could take. The show was this Saturday—just two days away. She would have to tell Rachel in school tomorrow—even if it ruined both of her New Year's resolutions!

"Rachel," Michelle whispered to herself at breakfast the next morning. She was practicing how she would tell Rachel about the penguin suit. "Rachel, remember how you said you wanted to skate in rhinestones and velvet and feathers? Well, you were right about the feathers."

"I can't believe my bad luck," Stephanie interrupted as she sat down at the table. "What was I thinking?"

"What's wrong, Steph?" Danny asked as

he put a plate of cranberry muffins on the table.

"The Back Yard Boys concert is this Saturday night," Stephanie said. "The same night as the opening night of the school play that my friends and I are in. I got the tickets for the wrong date!"

"What are you going to do?" Danny asked.

"I have no choice," Stephanie sighed. "I have to give the tickets to someone else."

"Don't look at me," Danny joked. "The only Back Yard Boys I know are the ones who mow our lawn."

"Cute, Dad," Stephanie said. "This is serious!"

Michelle looked up from her cereal bowl. Rachel's favorite group was the Back Yard Boys and Saturday was the same night as Yuks on Ice!

I'm saved! Michelle thought. If Rachel takes the tickets then she can't skate on Saturday night. And she'll never have to know about the penguin suit!

"Stephanie?" Michelle asked. "I think I know someone who would *love* those tickets."

"Ta-daaa!" Michelle sang. She waved three yellow tickets in front of Rachel's face in the school yard. "Tickets for the Back Yard Boys concert!"

Cassie and Mandy stood next to Michelle. They were nodding and grinning, trying to help Michelle give the tickets to Rachel.

"In the first row!" Mandy said.

"Right in the middle!" Cassie added.

"Show-offs," Rachel muttered. She began to leave, but Michelle grabbed her arm.

"No, Rachel, wait," Michelle said. "I want to give them to you!"

Rachel looked over her shoulder. "Me?"

"My sister Stephanie can't go," Michelle

said. "And I know how much you like the Back Yard Boys."

"More than anything," Rachel declared. "I named all my goldfish after them."

"Then go for it," Mandy said.

Rachel stared at the tickets. Then she raised one eyebrow and stared at Michelle. "Are you sure you want to give them to me? Why?"

"Because I want to do nice things for people, that's why!" Michelle said. "And all you have to do is be at the concert Saturday night at seven-thirty sharp."

"Saturday?" Rachel asked. "Wait a minute!" She narrowed her eyes at Michelle. "I can't go on Saturday!"

"Why not?" Michelle asked slowly.

"Duh-uh!" Rachel cried. "That's my big night! And now my father's company wants to sponsor the Yuks on Ice show. He even got some newspapers to come and take pictures!"

"Newspapers?" Mandy gasped.

Rachel threw back her shoulders proudly. "He's even serving free pies at the event. Cream pies!"

Michelle shuddered as she pictured one of the pies flying right into Rachel's face.

"But Rachel, the Back Yard Boys are coming to San Francisco only once this whole year!" Cassie cried. "How often will you have the chance to see them?"

"And how often will I have the chance to star in an ice show?" Rachel asked. She twirled a strand of her hair between her fingers. "Oh, and guess what?"

"There's more?" Mandy moaned.

Rachel nodded. "The Yuks committee called to tell me that my costume is ready," she said. "I'm picking it up tomorrow afternoon."

Michelle felt her body stiffen. "Did they tell you what kind of costume it is?" she asked.

Rachel shook her head. "They wanted to,

but I said no. I want it to be a surprise." She turned to leave.

Michelle stood frozen as she watched Rachel run over to Sidney. "Oh, it will be a surprise—a big one." she said. "That's for sure."

Chapter
8

♥ "You haven't told Rachel yet?" Mandy asked Michelle on Saturday morning.

"Not even last night?" Cassie asked.

Michelle shook her head as she stepped out of her house. She sat down on the doorstep with her friends.

"I tried," Michelle said. She put her elbows on her knees and rested her chin in her hands. "But Rachel's phone was busy all night. She was probably inviting everybody to the show."

"So what are you going to do now?" Mandy asked.

"I'm going to tell Rachel today," Michelle groaned. "Before she picks up her costume and flips."

"We'd better go with you," Cassie insisted.

"In case she flips anyway," Mandy said.

Michelle and her friends walked all the way to Rachel's house. The big white house was at the top of a steep hill. Michelle rang the doorbell.

"Yes?" a woman in a gray uniform asked as she opened the door. Michelle guessed she was the housekeeper.

"Hello," Michelle said politely. "Is Rachel home?"

The housekeeper smiled. "Yes, and you're just in time. Rachel is about to pick up her costume. She's so excited."

The girls waited while the housekeeper

called Rachel. Michelle could hear feet pounding down the stairs.

"Thanks, Leona," Rachel told the housekeeper. She stood at the door and smiled. "What's up?"

Michelle stared at Rachel. Just take a long, deep breath, she thought. And spit it out. "Joey told me what kind of costume you're wearing. It's not velvet, or rhinestones, or even lace."

Rachel shrugged. "Silk is nice."

"It's not silk, either," Michelle said. "It's . . . it's . . . it's a penguin suit!"

Michelle gave a little gasp. After all these days, she couldn't believe it was finally out!

"A penguin?" Rachel squeaked. "They want me to be a skating . . . *penguin?*"

Michelle forced herself to smile. "It's a huge part of the show, Rachel. No one else will be wearing a costume—only you!"

Rachel stared at Michelle. She didn't say a word.

"I could be the penguin if you don't want to do it anymore," Michelle told her.

Rachel folded her arms across her chest. "Liar, liar, pants on fire!" she exclaimed.

"What?" Michelle asked.

"I think you're making the whole thing up," Rachel said. "So I won't want to go and you'll have your old job back."

Michelle shook her head. "That's not true."

"Oh, yes, it is," Rachel said. "You know how much I hate penguins. And now that my dad has newspaper reporters coming, I bet you want your picture taken instead of mine."

Michelle was about to protest when Mrs. Tilly called for Rachel.

"I have to go now," Rachel said. "To pick up my real costume! The one with the velvet! And rhinestones! And feathers!"

Michelle jumped as Rachel slammed the door.

"It looks like Rachel is going to be a penguin tonight," Mandy said in a low voice.

"Yeah," Michelle groaned. "And I'm going to feel like a *turkey!*"

Michelle was too upset to do anything the rest of the afternoon. She just moped at home with Comet.

"Maybe Rachel has a better sense of humor than I thought, Comet," Michelle said as she stroked his soft fur. "Maybe the penguin suit will make her laugh."

The doorbell rang, and Comet barked. Michelle got up slowly and opened the door. Then she gasped.

Standing at the door in a big black and white penguin suit was Rachel Tilly—and she was *not* laughing.

"Well, you got your wish, Michelle!"

Rachel cried. "I'm going to make a fool of myself!"

Michelle stared at Rachel. The feathered suit had two black wings covering her arms. There was a short black tail and a hood with a pointy yellow beak attached to it.

"But I don't want you to make a fool of yourself," Michelle told Rachel. "I wanted us to be friends."

Comet squeezed past Michelle and began barking at Rachel.

"Go away!" Rachel said, flapping her wings at him.

Comet wagged his tail. Then he leaped toward Rachel and tried to catch one of her wings in his mouth.

Comet thinks she's playing with him, Michelle thought. "Comet, no!" she cried.

He didn't listen. Instead he leaped at Rachel, trying to grab her beak. Rachel gave a little cry and jumped off the doorstep. "I'll

65

get you for this, Michelle!" she shouted.

"WOOOOOOOOF!" Comet barked, and chased after Rachel. "Woof! Woof!"

Michelle gasped as Rachel flapped around the yard with Comet close behind her. "I—I was just trying to be nice!"

Chapter

9

♥ "Joey?" Michelle asked in the car that night. She was sitting between Cassie and Mandy in the back seat. Joey was driving them to the Diamond Rink. "What if all the air conditioners break down? And all the ice melts to slush? Will the show still go on?"

"You bet!" Joey said as they turned a corner. "But instead of Yuks on Ice, it'll be Yuks in Muck!"

"That's gross," Mandy said.

"No, it's not." Joey smiled. "That's just show biz!"

When they stopped for a traffic light, Joey

glanced over his shoulder. "By the way, Michelle," he said. "Why did you bring your ice skates?"

Michelle glanced down at the new skates in her lap. "In case Rachel needs help picking up the flowers and stuff."

"Wow," Joey said, smiling into the rearview mirror. "You really are doing nice things for people this year."

Michelle glanced at Mandy and Cassie. It was the least she could do for Rachel.

Joey did most of the talking as they drove to the Diamond Rink. He was wearing a black tuxedo with a red carnation stuck in the lapel. A pair of black ice skates lay on the seat next to him. "Here we are," he announced as he pulled into the parking lot.

Michelle looked out the car window. She had never seen the parking lot so full. Crowds of people were already lining up at the main entrance.

Joey parked the car. Then they all walked inside through the back door. Michelle gulped when she saw a big banner hanging over the rink. It read: TILLY PASTRIES PRESENTS YUKS ON ICE.

As they passed the snack stand, Michelle gulped again. Instead of the usual potato chips, cookies, and hot dogs, there were cream puffs, jelly doughnuts, and cream pies.

After tonight Rachel is never going to be able to look at one of her father's cream pies, Michelle thought. Not without thinking about what a bad friend I am. This is a nightmare!

A woman holding a clipboard led them into the locker room. It was bustling with excited comedians getting ready for the show.

"It's freezing in this place!" one man called out as he tied up his skates.

"What do you expect, Sid?" a woman said back. "It's a skating rink."

Joey went off to talk to one of the other comedians. Michelle looked around the locker room for a big black and white penguin.

"Do you see her?" Mandy whispered.

"Nope," Michelle whispered back.

Every time the locker room door opened, Michelle whirled around. But Rachel was nowhere to be found.

"It's showtime, you guys!" Joey announced to the other comedians. "I won't tell you to break a leg—because you probably will!"

"What is this guy, a comedian?" a woman with ice skates and a feather boa joked.

Music played as the girls followed Joey out to the skating rink. A young man wearing a baseball cap tossed a microphone to him. "You're on, Joey!" he said.

"Good luck," Michelle said. She held on tightly to her ice skates.

Joey gave Michelle a thumbs-up sign and skated onto the ice. The audience applauded as a spotlight followed Joey to the middle of the rink.

"Good evening, ladies and gentlemen!" Joey called out. "Tonight you'll have the pleasure of seeing some skaters perform a triple lutz. Or in my case . . . a single klutz!"

Cassie and Mandy laughed, but Michelle couldn't. Especially when the first skater was ready to go on and there was still no sign of Rachel.

"And now," Joey continued, "let's give a warm welcome for Michael Lobetsky as he skates to my favorite tune and yours—'Send in the Clowns.'"

A comedian wearing a rainbow wig and a rubber nose hobbled past the girls on his skates. The audience clapped as he skated shakily onto the ice.

71

"Where's Rachel?" Joey asked Michelle as soon as he got off the ice. "We need her soon!"

"I don't know, Joey," Michelle said.

"Well, she'd better show up," Joey said, heading for the locker room. "Or I'm on thin ice!"

"What if Rachel *doesn't* show up?" Michelle asked her friends.

"Then you take her place, Michelle," Mandy replied.

"Yeah, Michelle," Cassie said. "You'd better start putting on your skates."

"But I don't have a penguin suit!" Michelle wailed as she pulled her skates on.

Mandy looked around at all the comedians' props. She grabbed a fake arrow through the head and slipped it on Michelle.

"Wear this," she said. "It's funny!"

Michelle could hear her heart pound as the first skater finished his act. As he took a bow, flowers, teddy bears, and other stuffed animals came flying onto the ice.

Now what? Michelle wondered.

"Hey, you!" a gruff voice called. "You're on!"

Michelle gulped extra hard. "Who . . . me?"

Chapter 10

♡ "Not you!" a voice cried out.

Michelle spun around. Rachel was standing behind her, wearing the penguin suit—and a big scowl.

"Me!" Rachel snapped. Her long black penguin wings swept against Michelle as she pushed past her. "I'm doing this only because my dad says I have to."

Everyone backed away from the gate as Rachel stepped onto the ice. Michelle gulped when she heard the audience laugh at Rachel.

"I can't look!" She squeezed her eyes shut. "I can't look!"

"Yes, you can, Michelle," Cassie said, tugging at Michelle's arm. "We have to give Rachel our support."

Michelle, Cassie, and Mandy went up to the edge of the rink. They watched as Rachel skated around picking up the flowers and other gifts.

A comedian skated after Rachel with a bag of fake snow. The audience roared as he tossed handfuls of snow all over Rachel's head.

"Maybe Rachel will be a good sport," Michelle said hopefully. She held her breath as Rachel lugged the armful of flowers and teddy bears off the ice.

"You were great, Rachel," Michelle said, trying to smile.

Rachel glared at Michelle. Then she shoved the pile of gifts against Michelle's chest.

"I was never so embarrassed in my life!"

Michelle watched as Rachel waddled back to the locker room.

"It's got to get better," Mandy said.

But it only got worse.

The audience laughed harder and louder each time Rachel skated onto the ice. More and more comedians began skating after Rachel, too. One even flapped his arms and made penguin noises.

"It can't get worse than this!" Michelle buried her face in her hands. "It just can't!"

"Oh, yes, it can," Mandy said. "Did you tell Rachel about the cream pie?"

"Huh?" Michelle looked up. She had totally forgotten about the pie!

The last skater took her bow. Rachel skated around the ice, picking up flowers and teddy bears. Then Michelle saw Joey standing at the gate. He was balancing a cream pie in his hand.

"No, Joey!" Michelle shouted. "Wait!"

It was too late. Joey didn't hear Michelle. He inched his way onto the ice.

"I've got to stop him!" Michelle cried. "Rachel's been embarrassed too much already!" Still wearing the arrow on her head, she pushed her way onto the ice.

"Stop, Joey!" Michelle shouted.

The audience went wild as Michelle speeded across the ice.

Joey turned on his skates with the pie in his hand.

"Michelle?" he asked.

Michelle stopped pumping her arms and legs. She held her breath as she let herself glide past Joey.

"Gotcha!" Michelle cried as she snatched the cream pie out of Joey's hand. She turned on her blades and saw Rachel whizzing in her direction in the penguin suit. At least I stopped Rachel from getting a pie in the face, she thought.

Then Michelle moved to skate away. The toe of her blade caught on a rose that had landed nearby.

"W-w-w-whoa!" Michelle cried as she lost her balance. She fell forward and—

SPLAT!

The cream pie hit Rachel right in the face!

Chapter 11

♥ The Diamond Rink was so quiet you could hear a snowflake drop.

Michelle gaped at Rachel as she spit and sputtered. She reached up and wiped whipped cream off her penguin eyes. A big clump of custard plopped from her beak.

"I—I—I was just trying to be nice," Michelle stammered. She skated backward as Rachel slowly skated forward.

Michelle gulped when Rachel pulled off her penguin hood. Rachel's face was red and angry.

Planting her hands on her hips, Rachel

glared at Michelle. She opened her mouth to speak. But before any angry words came out, something amazing happened—the audience began to cheer!

"Pen-guin! Pen-guin! Pen-guin!"

Michelle couldn't believe her ears. The whole Diamond Rink seemed to shake as people clapped their hands and stomped their feet.

And it was all for Rachel!

"Penguin?" Rachel gasped. "That's me!"

Michelle smiled at Rachel.

"They like me!" Rachel gushed. "They really like me!"

"Pen-guin! Pen-guin! Pen-guin!"

With a sweep of her arm Rachel tossed her penguin hood to Michelle. Then she took a long, deep bow.

A warm spotlight fell on Rachel. Soft music filled the rink as Rachel began performing a perfect sit-spin!

"How do you like that?" Joey joked to

Michelle. "And I thought I was the star!"

Michelle gave Joey a little shrug. "That's just show biz!" She giggled.

Michelle looked over at Cassie and Mandy and waved at them. She was happy with the way things had turned out. And she had a pretty good idea that Rachel was, too!

"Good morning, Michelle," Danny said cheerfully the next day. He was whipping up a batch of his special Sunday morning waffles. "Do you want whipped cream on your waffles?"

"Whipped cream?" Michelle asked. She thought of Rachel dripping with cream and began to giggle. "I think I'll just stick to syrup, Dad."

The doorbell rang, and Michelle ran to open it. Standing on the doorstep was Rachel. She held a newspaper in one hand and a small shopping bag in the other.

"Ta-daaa!" Rachel sang. She held the newspaper up in front of Michelle's face. "Check it out, Michelle!"

Michelle stared at the picture on the front page. It was of Rachel in her penguin suit doing her sit-spin!

"Read it!" Rachel waved the paper excitedly.

"'The ice may have been cold,'" Michelle read out loud, "'but Rachel Tilly warmed everyone's heart.'"

Michelle smiled. Rachel's dream had come true, and Michelle had helped!

"You did something nice for me." Rachel handed Michelle the shopping bag. "And now I'm going to do something nice for you!"

Michelle peeked into Rachel's bag. It was filled with her dad's raspberry jelly doughnuts and blueberry muffins!

"Wait right here!" Michelle told Rachel. "Don't go away!"

Michelle ran into the house. She grabbed two cups and a container of milk. Then she and Rachel ran around to the backyard and spread the doughnuts and milk on a picnic table.

Just like friends, Michelle thought. Well . . . almost.

"Do you still hate penguins, Rachel?" Michelle asked as she grabbed a doughnut.

"Are you kidding?" Rachel asked through a mouthful of powdered sugar. "I *love* penguins. And guess what?"

"What?" Michelle asked.

"The Yuks told me I can keep all the teddy bears and flowers from last night," Rachel said. She heaved a big sigh. "Now if I can just figure out where to keep them."

"That's a lot of teddy bears," Michelle admitted. Then she had a thought. "I have an idea," she said. "Why don't you do something nice with the teddy bears and flowers?"

"Like what?" Rachel asked. Her eyes drifted up as she thought. Then she gave a little jump. "Hey, I know!" she said. "Every month my dad donates pastries and cakes to a local hospital. Maybe I can donate the flowers and teddy bears."

Michelle nodded. "The children can get the teddy bears, and the flowers can go to the other rooms!" she said excitedly.

"Yeah!" Rachel said. She began to stand up. "And I bet I'll get my picture in the newspaper again! Or be on TV!"

"Newspaper? TV?" Michelle's mouth dropped open. Was that stuff really more important to Rachel than helping people?

"Oh, well." Rachel sighed. "I'd better go home and start packing those teddy bears. Bye, Michelle!"

Michelle watched as Rachel practically skipped out of her yard. She shook her head and sighed.

Some things about Rachel Tilly will never, ever change, Michelle thought. But at least I got her to do something nice. And getting others to do nice things is just as good as doing them yourself.

Michelle reached for another doughnut and smiled. "It's going to be a very happy New Year!"

It doesn't matter if you live around the corner...
or around the world...
If you are a fan of Mary-Kate and Ashley Olsen,
you should be a member of

MARY-KATE + ASHLEY'S FUN CLUB™

Here's what you get:
Our Funzine™
An autographed color photo
Two black & white individual photos
A full size color poster
An official **Fun Club**™ membership card
A **Fun Club**™ school folder
Two special **Fun Club**™ surprises
A holiday card
Fun Club™ collectibles catalog
Plus a **Fun Club**™ box to keep everything in

To join Mary-Kate + Ashley's Fun Club™, fill out the form
below and send it along with

U.S. Residents – $17.00
Canadian Residents – $22 U.S. Funds
International Residents – $27 U.S. Funds

MARY-KATE + ASHLEY'S FUN CLUB™
859 HOLLYWOOD WAY, SUITE 275
BURBANK, CA 91505

NAME:_____

ADDRESS:_____

_CITY:_____ STATE:_____ ZIP:_____

PHONE:(___) _____ BIRTHDATE:_____

1242

FULL HOUSE™
Michelle

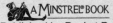
A MINSTREL® BOOK
Published by Pocket Books

1033-34

Don't miss out on any of
Stephanie and Michelle's
exciting adventures!

FULL HOUSE™
Sisters

When sisters get together...
expect the unexpected!

A MINSTREL® BOOK

Published by Pocket Books

2012-05